WAR GAME

"PUNCH," OCTOBER 21, 1914.

THE GREATER GAME.

MR. PUNCH (*to Professional Association Player*). "NO DOUBT YOU CAN MAKE MONEY IN THIS FIELD, MY FRIEND, BUT THERE'S ONLY ONE FIELD TO-DAY WHERE YOU CAN GET HONOUR."

WAR GAME

MICHAEL FOREMAN

PAVILION

In memory of my uncles, who died in the Great War.
William James Foreman, killed aged 18
Frederick Benjamin Foreman, killed aged 20
William Henry Goddard, killed aged 20
Lacey Christmas Goddard, died of wounds Christmas Day 1918 aged 24

This edition published in Great Britain in 1997 by
PAVILION BOOKS LIMITED
London House, Great Eastern Wharf, Parkgate Road, London SW11 4NQ
The moral right of the author has been asserted.
Text and illustrations copyright © Michael Foreman 1993
Designed by Janet James

A CIP catalogue record for this book is available from the
British Library.

ISBN 1 85793 713 9

Printed and bound in Italy by Giunti, Prato

4 6 8 10 9 7 5

This book may be ordered by post direct from the publisher. Please contact
the Marketing Department. But try your bookshop first.

The publishers would like to thank the following for permission to reproduce
illustrative material: Bowman Gray Collection, University of North Carolina at
Chapel Hill pp. 2, 8, 12, 26, 36 and endpapers; Hulton Picture Library p. 7;
Imperial War Museum p. 9; British Library Newspaper Library pp. 10
(bottom), 57; Tonie & Valmai Holt pp. 10 (top), 46; Mansell Collection p. 12;
John Frost Historical Newspaper Collection pp. 12, 57.

THE KICK-OFF

GOAL! Will saw the ball hit the back of the net. In his imagination he had just scored for England, and he heard the roar of a huge crowd. But he knew that around the pitch there was no crowd, just a low hedge and the familiar flat fields of the Suffolk countryside.

A group of small boys jumped around behind the goal and a few old men sitting under the elms clapped. The church clock struck five. The game was over.

The two teams changed and joked together. 'We'll come back and beat you after the war,' laughed one of the opposing team as they began their walk back to their village five miles away.

'Most of them are joining the army,' said Freddie, the goalkeeper. 'We should, really.'

'I'd like to,' said Billy, eyes shining with excitement.

'No, you're too young. If you went, I'd have to go to look after you,' laughed his big brother Lacey.

'It *would* be an adventure, though,' said Will. 'And they say it'll be over by Christmas. Be a pity to miss it.'

And so they talked as they wandered back along the dusty lane into the village.

The summer of 1914 had been one of the hottest ever, and while Will and his friends had worked long and hard in the harvest fields, far away in a place called Sarajevo an Archduke had been killed. The German emperor, Kaiser Bill, was using the confusion as an excuse to start a war and seize territory from his neighbouring countries.

'So once again the British Army has to go overseas and sort things out,' said the old men of the village over their pints of beer.

Many of the old soldiers of the village had already been recalled to the army and were on their way to the battlefields of France and Belgium. There was a lot of pressure on the young men to follow them. The British Army needed many thousands of men to stop the Germans advancing across Europe. Recruitment posters were everywhere, and the newspapers called on every man to do his duty 'for King and Country'.

THE VETERAN'S FAREWELL.

"Good Bye, my lad,
I only wish I were young enough
to go with you!"

ENLIST NOW!

The day after the football match was a Sunday, and the vicar boomed out the same message from his pulpit. The local squire, in the front pew, wore all the medals he could get his hands on, and his son wore a brand-new, tailor-made officer's uniform. After the service, Will, Freddie, Billy and Lacey sat by the signpost under the oak and the elm at the corner of the green. Here they had sat almost every day of their lives, after church, after school and after work.

'I think we should join,' said Freddie. 'None of us has even been outside the county. It's time we saw something of the world.'

'Yes! An adventure – and home by Christmas,' said Billy.

Will wasn't so sure. After all, he thought, a lot of people can get killed in a war. But they agreed that next day after work, they would go into town and see what was happening at the Town Hall, the local army recruiting office.

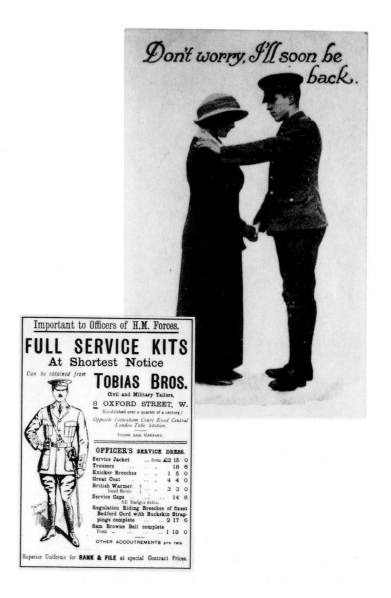

THE ADVENTURE

They had never seen such a crowd. There was a great feeling of excitement and even of fun as the flags waved and the band played. Every time a lad went to join up, the crowd gave him a hearty cheer.

Before anyone could stop him, Billy was up the steps and the crowd was cheering him. Then Freddie followed. Lacey had to go to look after Billy. Will knew he couldn't let his friends go off to war without him, so to wild cheers all four joined the army. They were given railway warrants and told to report to barracks in four days' time.

They had a lot of explaining to do when they got home that evening.

Is One Dear to You Fighting in the Great War?

If so you are entitled to **WEAR THIS BADGE.**

SACRIFICE!

It is worn by women who have a relative or sweetheart serving.

Send 1/-

and the name of the one serving to; The Woman's Branch, National Service, 63, Temple Chambers, London, E.C.

The Pendant of Service and Sacrifice.

"We Must All Fall In," the National Service Marching Song, can be obtained (post free 7d.) from the same address.

---

4 Questions to the Women of England

1 YOU have read what the Germans have done in Belgium. Have you thought what they would do if they invaded England?

2 Do you realise that the Safety of your Home and Children depends on our getting more men now?

3 Do you realise that the one word "Go" from you may send another man to fight for our King and Country?

4 When the War is over and your husband or your son is asked, "What did you do in the great War?"—is he to hang his head because you would not let him go?

Women of England do your duty! Send your men to-day to join our glorious Army.

God Save the King.

---

4 Questions to Clerks and Shop Assistants.

1. If you are between 19 and 38 years of age, are you really satisfied with what you are doing to-day?

2. Do you feel happy as you walk along the streets and see brave men in khaki who are going to fight for the Empire while you stay at home in comfort?

3. Do you realise that our gallant fellows are giving up everything on your behalf, to save you, your women and your womenfolk?

Ask your employer to-day to be allowed to enlist?

He will keep your position open for you and so help the Empire?

Do this thing by you—your employers are helping.

ENLIST NOW AND FIGHT TO-DAY.

God Save THE KING.

---

5 Questions to patriotic Shopkeepers

1. HAVE you any fit men between 19 and 38 years of age serving behind your counter who at this moment ought to be serving their country?

2. Will you call your male employees together and explain to them that in order to end the War quickly we must have more men?

3. Will you tell them what you are prepared to do for them whilst they are fighting for the Empire?

4. Have you realised that we cannot have "business as usual" whilst the War continues?

    THE ARMY WANTS MORE MEN TO-DAY.

5. Could not Women or older men fill their places till the War is over?

YOUR COUNTRY WILL APPRECIATE THE HELP YOU GIVE

God Save the King.

DESIGNED BY LT. GEN. SIR R.S.S BADEN POWELL

Are <u>YOU</u> in this?

Being country boys, they were all good shots, and they were signed into the Kings Royal Rifles. It sounded very grand. But so great was the rush to join that the army was overwhelmed with recruits and didn't have enough uniforms for them all. Will and the other lads were disappointed and felt foolish learning the basic training and drills wearing their ordinary clothes. They slept in bell tents in a huge field, about a dozen men to a tent. The food was poor and the days were long and exhausting.

However, after a few weeks they were all kitted out and the 'adventure' had really started. They boarded a P&O ship in Southampton and prepared to set sail at six o'clock in a great convoy. The whole of Southampton turned out to see them off. Thousands of sailors cheered and waved their caps from destroyers in Southampton Water.

As the coast of England faded behind them, Will, like the countless young men crowded around him, felt strangely alone with his thoughts of home and of what lay over the horizon.

'Come on, lads. Let's have a song,' called Freddie. They sang as they sailed and felt better.

TO THE FRONT

When they reached France they were packed into trains, which stopped and started and crawled all day along the overcrowded tracks.

The country didn't look so different. People worked the fields just as the lads had done back home. Some of the workers unbent their backs and waved as the trains went by.

The soldiers finally arrived at a small station that had grown into a vast supply depot. Trains and trucks were being shunted and unloaded. Mountains of stores, horse lines and mule lines were everywhere, and there was a babel of shouted commands.

Then at last they were off the trains and marching. Will felt good to be out in the fresh air and swinging along with his mates. Marching through villages and towns, the troops were cheered all the way. Flowers, fruit and bread were pressed into their arms. It seemed like a pretty good war so far, even though it had begun to rain and the long dry summer was over.

Then things began to change. The roads became crowded with people moving back from the Front. The whole population seemed to be on the move. Families carried their children and pushed prams loaded with whatever they could salvage from their lives. No more cheering crowds. These people had seen war. Their homes had been blown to bits, their farms criss-crossed by armies, trenches, wire, and pock-marked by a million artillery shells. Will could hear the almost continuous sound of shellfire in the distance.

They passed wagons full of wounded soldiers on their way back to England, and long lines of exhausted ragged troops sitting in the mud, rain and gathering darkness before being ordered back into the action.

At last the marching came to an end, and Will, Freddie, Lacey and Billy and the rest of the brigade were ordered on to a fleet of London General omnibuses that were to rush them up to the Front to fill a gap in the 'Line'. They drove through the ruins of a devastated town. The lads had never been to London, yet here they were riding on a London bus in the middle of France. The conductor's bell was still working, and one of the men kept ringing it and shouting 'Next stop Piccadilly Circus!' The glassless windows were covered with boards, but there were plenty of holes to peep through. Will's first reaction was: 'Doesn't it look pretty? Just like fireworks.'

Then they were in the trenches. Not the front trench, but the reserve. In single file they moved forward along a winding communication trench to the support trench. Here they waited with the sound of battle exploding all around them.

There was a lull.

'All right, lads. It's our turn,' said their sergeant, and in single file and pouring rain they squelched along another communication trench to the Front.

The trenches of the Western Front crossed Belgium and France for a distance of 460 miles. The Front trench was about three feet wide at the bottom and seven feet high. To enable the soldiers to fire over or through the parapet, a fire-step was built two feet high into the forward side of the trench. It was on this that the sentries stood to keep watch.

Lavatories, or latrines, were dug at the end of short trenches, mostly to the rear of the main trench. Occasionally they were dug a little way forward into No Man's Land to discourage anyone from lingering too long.

There was still no shooting on this section of the Line as Will and his mates crouched on the fire-step to allow wounded and exhausted soldiers to pass by on their way to the rear.

EVEN A DOG ENLISTS
WHY NOT YOU?
660 MARKET ST. SAN FRANCISCO
Or any U.S. Army Recruiting Station

Dogs were sometimes used as sentries in some sections, particularly by the French. Some dogs also searched for wounded men and others were messenger dogs.

NO MAN'S LAND

Will and Freddie were the first to be posted as sentries on their little section, and, cautiously, they stood up on the fire-step. They peered over the parapet into No Man's Land. They could just see their own first line of wire and random humps and bumps in an otherwise flat landscape that seeped rapidly into darkness. A landscape as flat as the fields of home.

Then a flare arced and spiralled slowly from the sky. Will and Freddie could see that the humps and bumps were men. Dead men. Some of them, who had cut their trousers into shorts during the hot weather, looked like fallen schoolboys.

Before the flare faded, Will and Freddie saw more lines of wire and, beyond No Man's Land, the front line of German trenches.

'Less than a goal kick away,' whispered Freddie.

The newcomers quickly learned the routine of trench life. An hour before dawn every morning they received the order to 'Stand To'. Half asleep and frozen, the men climbed on to the fire-step, rifles clutched with numb fingers and bayonets fixed.

The half light of dawn and at dusk was when an attack was most expected, and both sides had their trenches fully manned at those times. Sometimes nothing happened. Often there was a furious exchange of rifle and machine-gun fire to discourage any attack through the gloom. This was known as 'morning hate'.

After an hour or so the order was given to 'Stand Down'. Only the sentries remained on the fire-step and the rest of the men enjoyed what breakfast they could get among the rats, blood-red slugs and horned beetles that infested the trenches.

Each company going to the Front Line took food for three days, usually bully beef, tins of jam and bone-hard biscuit. Army biscuit had to be smashed with a shovel or bayonet. The pieces were then soaked in water for a couple of days and were sometimes added to soup.

Dugouts were dug into the sides of trenches and roofed with timber or corrugated iron and covered with a minimum of 9 inches of earth and sandbags.

Sometimes the rats would suddenly disappear. Old soldiers thought this to be a sure sign of imminent heavy shelling.

As the weather grew worse, the two huge armies became bogged down in virtually fixed positions. In some places they were only thirty yards apart, so close that the heavy guns, firing from behind the reserve lines, often killed their own men when shells fell short of their target.

The mud became deeper and deeper as thousands of men, mules, horses and heavy wagons and guns churned it up.

Now and then the soldiers were ordered to attack across No Man's Land, even though many lives were always lost and little or nothing was achieved. Small raiding parties ventured out at night to cause as much damage as they could, and, if possible, to return with a prisoner or two who could provide some useful information. Other small teams were sent to repair or lay new wire. The covering darkness could be suddenly illuminated at any time by flares. A pistol flare remained bright for about fifteen seconds. This seemed an eternity to men lying motionless in No Man's Land awaiting the rattle of machine-gun fire or a sniper's bullet.

The Germans sometimes used a flare suspended from a small parachute. This blazed brightly for up to a minute, and might be followed by a second and a third flare.

"TUBS FOR TOMMIES".

£10 WILL PROVIDE A UNIT OF 4 BATHS. WITH STOVE, BOILER, TOWELS, SOAP, SCRUBBERS AND ALL EQUIPMENT.

FROM THE EMERGENCY VOLUNTARY AID COMMITTEE OF THE EMPRESS CLUB DOVER STREET W.

SOAP

APPLY TO THE SECRETARY, BRANCH OFFICE, 36, QUEEN VICTORIA ST., E.C.

Steel helmets were devised in 1915. In short supply, they were passed from one man to another as the soldiers left the firing line. The Battle of the Somme in 1916 was the first time that all the British soldiers had their own helmets.

The communication trenches were particularly busy at night. Dead and wounded were carried to the rear, and food and munitions were brought to the Front. When possible the dead were recovered from No Man's Land. Like clearing the table after dinner, ready for the Generals' next game of soldiers, Will thought.

Will often thought of his family sleeping peacefully just 100 miles away, and of his own bed, dry and warm under the thatched eaves of home. Even his old dog guarding the yard and the pigs in the byre lived in more comfort than Will and the British Army.

And still it rained.

The water table of this flat land was often less than three feet below the surface. Every shell hole filled with water. The trenches were awash with mud. Here and there men hollowed out little caves or 'scrapes' in the sides of the trenches to give them some protection from the rain, but they had little protection from the high-explosive shells, which could rain down at any moment.

The enemy trenches were so close that whenever the fighting died down, each army could hear the other's voices and could sometimes even smell their breakfast. They all knew that they were sharing the same terrible conditions.

Singing in the trenches was common in 1914, and songs from one front line floated to the other on the quiet evening air. Occasionally during a quiet period a British Tommie would put a tin can on a stick and hold it above the parapet to give the Germans some shooting practice. The Germans would do likewise with tin cans or bottles, and a shooting match would develop accompanied by cheers and boos.

Sometimes the soldiers watched rival aircraft confront each other in mid-air duels over the trenches.

Will, Freddie, Lacey and Billy stayed together as much as possible and lived like bedraggled moles in a world of mud, attack and counter-attack.

The weather, still wet, grew steadily colder. Then, one night, as the lads returned to the Front after a few days' rest, the rain stopped and it grew bitterly cold.

That night they were relieving a Scottish regiment, and as the Scots left the Line, the Germans shouted Christmas wishes to them.

The primitive warplanes of 1914 were not armed at first and flew on spy missions, spotting enemy gun positions, supply depots and troop movements.

Pilot and observer were usually armed with revolver and rifle respectively. Some carried grenades, which they tried to drop on to the trenches.

Then tiny lights appeared in the German trenches. As far as the eye could see, Christmas trees were flickering along the parapet of the German lines.

It was Christmas Eve.

A single German voice began to sing 'Silent Night'. It was joined by many others.

The British replied with 'The First Noel' to applause from the Germans. And so it went on, turn and turn about. Then both front lines sang 'O Come All Ye Faithful'.

It was a beautiful moonlit night. Occasionally a star shell hung like a Star of Bethlehem.

At dawn, when the British were all 'Stood To' on the fire-step, they saw a world white with frost. The few shattered trees that remained were white. Lines of wire glinted like tinsel. The humps of dead in No Man's Land were like toppled snowmen.

After the singing of the night, the Christmas dawn was strangely quiet. The clock of death had stopped ticking.

Then a German climbed from his trench and planted a Christmas tree in No Man's Land. Freddie, being a goalkeeper and therefore a bit daft, walked out and shook hands with him. Both sides applauded.

A small group of men from each side, unarmed, joined them. They all shook hands. One of the Germans spoke good English and said he hoped the war would end soon because he wanted to return to his job as a taxi driver in Birmingham.

It was agreed that they should take the opportunity to bury the dead. The bodies were mixed up together. They were sorted out, and a joint burial service was held on the 'halfway line'.

Both sides then returned to their trenches for breakfast. Will and the lads were cheered by the wonderful smell of bacon, and they had a hot breakfast for a change.

One by one, birds began to arrive from all sides. The soldiers hardly ever saw a bird normally, but Will counted at least fifty sparrows hopping around their trench.

Christmas presents for the men consisted of a packet of chocolate, Oxo cubes, a khaki handkerchief, peppermints, camp cocoa, writing paper and a pencil. After breakfast a pair of horses and a wagon arrived with Princess Mary's Christmas gifts – a pipe and tobacco and a Christmas card from the King and Queen.

With our best wishes for Christmas 1914 May God protect you and bring you home safe

Mary R   George R.I.

There were no planes overhead, no observation balloons, no bombs, no rifle fire, no snipers, just an occasional skylark. The early mist lifted to reveal a clear blue sky. The Germans were strolling about on their parapet once more, and waved to the British to join them. Soon there was quite a crowd in No Man's Land. Both sides exchanged small gifts. One German had been a barber in Holborn in London. A chair was placed on the 'halfway line', and he gave haircuts to several of the British soldiers.

Then, from somewhere, a football bounced across the frozen mud. Will was on it in a flash. He trapped the ball with his left foot, flipped it up with his right, and headed it towards Freddie.

Freddie made a spectacular dive, caught the ball in both hands and threw it to a group of Germans.

Immediately a vast, fast and furious football match was underway. Goals were marked by caps. Freddie, of course, was in one goal and a huge German in the other.

Apart from that, it was wonderfully disorganized, part football, part ice-skating, with unknown numbers on each team. No referee, no account of the score.

It was just terrific to be no longer an army of moles, but up and running on top of the ground that had threatened to entomb them for so long. And this time Will really could hear a big crowd – and he *was* playing for England!

He was playing in his usual centre forward position with Lacey to his left and little Billy on the wing. The game surged back and forth across No Man's Land. The goalposts grew larger as greatcoats and tunics were discarded as the players warmed to the sport. Khaki and grey mixed together. Steam rose from their backs, and their faces were wreathed in smiles and clouds of breath in the clear frosty air.

Some of the British officers took a dim view of
such sport, and when the game came to its
exhausted end, the men were encouraged back to
their trenches for a carol service and supper. The
haunting sound of men singing drifted back and
forth across No Man's Land in the still night air.

'Good night, Tommies. See you tomorrow.'

'Good night, Fritz. We'll have another game.'

But Boxing Day passed without a game. The officers were alarmed at what had happened on Christmas Day. If such friendly relations continued, how could they get the men to fight again? How could the war continue?

The men were not allowed to leave the trenches. There were a few secret meetings here and there along the Front, and gifts and souvenirs were exchanged.

It was the Duke of Wellington who gave the nickname 'Tommie' to the British soldiers. When asked in 1843 to think of a name typical of the private soldier, the great duke thought back over his long career to his first campaign in the Low Countries. He remembered a group of wounded men lying on the ground. One of them had a sabre slash in his head, a bayonet wound in his chest, and a bullet through his lungs. He begged not to be moved, but to be left to die in peace. He must have seen Wellington's concern. 'It's all right, sir,' he gasped. 'It's all in the day's work.'
'What's your name, soldier?' the Duke asked.
'Thomas Atkins, sir.'
They were his last words.

Two more days passed peacefully. Then a message was thrown over from the German side. A very important general was due to visit their section at 3.15 that afternoon and he would want to see some action. The Germans therefore would start firing at 3 pm and the Tommies should please keep their heads down.

At three o'clock a few warning shots were fired over the British trenches and then heavy fire lasted for an hour. The Tommies kept their heads down.

At dawn a few days later, the Germans mounted a full-scale attack. The friendly Germans from Saxony had been withdrawn and replaced by fresh troops from Prussia. They were met by rapid and deadly fire from the British and were forced back.

The order was given to counter-attack, to try to take the German trenches before they could reorganize themselves. Will and the rest of the British soldiers scrambled over the parapet.

Freddie still had the football! He drop-kicked it far into the mist of No Man's Land.
'That'll give someone a surprise,' he said.
'Why are goalies always daft?' thought Will.

They were on the attack. Running in a line, Will in a centre forward position, Lacey to his left, young Billy on the wing.

From the corner of his eye Will saw Freddie dive full-length, then curl up as if clutching a ball in the best goalkeeping tradition.

'Daft as a brush,' Will thought.

Suddenly they all seemed to be tackled at once. The whole line went down. Earth and sky turned over, and Will found himself in a shell hole staring at the sky. Then everything went black.

Slowly the blackness cleared and Will could see
the hazy sky once more. Bits of him felt hot and
other bits felt very cold. He couldn't move his legs.
He heard a slight movement. There was someone
else in the shell hole.

Will dimly recognized the gleam of a fixed
bayonet and the outline of a German.

'*Wasser. Wasser,*' the German said.

It was about the only German word Will knew.
He fumbled for his water bottle and managed to
push it towards the German with the butt of his
rifle.

The German drank deeply. He didn't have the
strength to return the bottle.

'*Kinder*?' he said. Will shook his head. The
German held up three fingers. Will tried to shake
his head again to show that he did not understand,
but the blackness returned.

Later he saw a pale ball of gold in the misty sky. 'There's a ball in Heaven,' he thought. 'Thank God.
We'll all have a game when this nightmare's over.'

At home when he had a bad dream he knew that if he opened his eyes, the bad dream would end.
But here, his eyes were already open.

Perhaps if he closed them, the nightmare would end.

He closed his eyes.